Click, Clack
Rainy Day

For Esmé
—D. C.

For Ted,
Thanks for the rainbow.
—B. L.

SIMON SPOTLIGHT
An imprint of Simon & Schuster Children's Publishing Division
1230 Avenue of the Americas, New York, New York 10020
This Simon Spotlight edition May 2022
Text copyright © 2022 by Doreen Cronin
Illustrations copyright © 2022 by Betsy Lewin
All rights reserved, including the right of reproduction in whole or in part in any form.
SIMON SPOTLIGHT, READY-TO-READ, and colophon are registered trademarks of Simon & Schuster, Inc.
For information about special discounts for bulk purchases, please contact Simon & Schuster Special Sales
at 1-866-506-1949 or business@simonandschuster.com.
Manufactured in the United States of America 0322 LAK
10 9 8 7 6 5 4 3 2 1
Library of Congress Cataloging-in-Publication Data
Names: Cronin, Doreen, author. | Lewin, Betsy, illustrator. Title: Click, clack rainy day / by Doreen Cronin ;
illustrated by Betsy Lewin. Other titles: Rainy day Description: New York : Simon Spotlight, 2022. |
Series: A click, clack book | Summary: On a rainy day, everyone on the farm stays inside except the cows,
who enjoy the rain, mud, and wind. Identifiers: LCCN 2021041129 | ISBN 9781665911146 (pbk) |
ISBN 9781665911153 (hc) | ISBN 9781665911160 (ebook) Subjects: CYAC: Rain and rainfall—Fiction. |
Domestic animals—Fiction. | Farmers—Fiction. | LCGFT: Picture books.
Classification: LCC PZ7.C88135 Cmm 2022 | DDC [E]—dc23
LC record available at https://lccn.loc.gov/2021041129

Click, Clack
Rainy Day

By Doreen Cronin

Illustrated by Betsy Lewin

Ready-to-Read

Simon Spotlight

New York London Toronto Sydney New Delhi

It is raining on the farm.
The rain rolls off the roof
of the house.

The rain rolls
off the roof
of the barn.

The rain rolls off the roof
of the tractor shed.

Farmer Brown stays in the house.
Farmer Brown does not like to be wet.

The rain makes a *drip* sound.
The rain makes a *drop* sound.
The rain makes a *drip-drop* sound
on the window.

The rain is falling harder.
The rain makes a puddle
in the pigpen.

The rain makes a puddle
in the driveway.

The rain makes a puddle
around the mailbox.

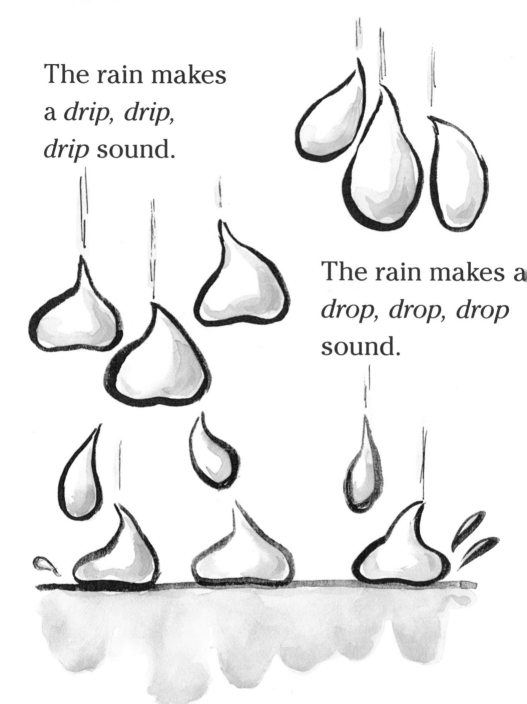

The rain makes
a *drip, drip,
drip* sound.

The rain makes a
drop, drop, drop
sound.

The rain makes a
*drip-drop, drip-drop,
drip-drop* sound on the barn roof.

The chickens stay in the barn.
The chickens do not like to be wet.

The mice stay in the barn.
The mice do not like to be wet.

The cows are outside.
The cows like to be wet.

They like the sound of the rain
on their heads.
They like the feel of the mud
on their feet.

Farmer Brown is worried about
the cows.
He brings them umbrellas
so their heads are not so wet.

Farmer Brown goes back
into the house.
He is a little bit wet now.

The chickens are worried
about the cows.
They bring them rain boots
so their feet are not so wet.

The chickens go back to the barn.
They are a little bit wet now.

The wind begins to blow.
The wind blows the weather vane
on the top of the barn.

The wind blows the leaves
on the big oak tree.

The wind blows the stalks
in the cornfield.

The mice are worried about the cows.
They bring them sweaters
to help them stay warm.

The mice go back to the barn.
They are a little bit wet now.

The cows are under umbrellas.
They hear the *drip-drop* of the rain.
They cannot feel the rain
on their heads.

The cows are in rain boots.
The rain rolls off the rubber boots.
They cannot feel the mud
on their feet.

The cows are wearing sweaters.
Nobody likes a wet sweater.

The wind begins to blow harder.
The wind spins the weather vane
on the barn.

The wind shakes the branches
of the big oak tree.

The wind bends the stalks
in the cornfield.

The wind blows away the umbrellas.
The cows can feel the rain
on their heads.

The wind blows away the wet sweaters.
The cows can feel the rain
on their skin.

The wind blows the cows
right out of their rain boots.

The cows blow past the window.

The cows blow past the barn.

Farmer Brown runs out
of the house.
The wind takes his hat.

The rain makes a *drip-drop, drip-drop,
drip-drop* sound on his head.

Everyone is wet.
Everyone feels the rain on their heads.
Everyone feels the mud on their feet.
Nobody wears a wet sweater.

Everybody loves the rain.

The cows land on their feet.

The mice run out of the barn.
The puddles are deep.
The wind is strong.

The chickens run out of the barn.
The rain rolls off their beaks.
The wind ruffles their feathers.
They pick up the mice.